This book belongs to

Acknowledgments
Special thanks to Lucasfilm Ltd for their invaluable assistance
and for providing the artwork for this book.

First published in the UK in 2024 by Studio Press Books,
an imprint of Bonnier Books UK,
4th Floor, Victoria House, Bloomsbury Square,
London WC1B 4DA
Owned by Bonnier Books,
Sveavägen 56, Stockholm, Sweden
bonnierbooks.co.uk

Printed in China
1 3 5 7 9 10 8 6 4 2

ISBN 978-1-80078-720-9

Text adapted by Tom Huddleston
Edited by Emil Fortune
Designed by Maddox Philpot
Cover illustrated by Alexander Ward
Production by Nick Read

A CIP catalogue record is available from the British Library

In late Spring of 1977, something profound happened. Star Wars: A New Hope *premiered, and it changed everything. It changed what movies could be, it changed the way movies were made, and it changed the way movies looked. The world had never seen anything like it.*

I was twelve years old when *Star Wars* released in theaters. I stood in line with the crowds and waited in anticipation once I took my seat. As soon as the score began to play and the *Star Wars* logo zoomed away from the audience, I was hooked. I was mesmerized by the now-famous crawl and the enormous Star Destroyer that kept going on and on for what felt like forever. Just those first few minutes of the film ignited the imaginations, creative trajectories, and career paths of me and so many other people: artists, model makers, writers, filmmakers, and more.

I watched the film five times in a row that day. I cheered for Luke, Han, and Leia – the farmboy, smuggler, and princess. I loved the comedic bantering of the droid duo of C-3PO and R2-D2, and it brought lightsabers, the Force, and Jedi into my life. I couldn't get enough of the design of Darth Vader and the stormtroopers with their helmets and armor. Everyone booed when Darth Vader came on screen, but I thought he was the coolest villain I had ever seen.

A New Hope gave us a new way to see and think about a story set in space. It did not look overly futuristic and it wasn't pristine. It was dirty and worn. It gave us a galaxy that looked used and 'lived in.' It gave us realism from the dents in the *Millennium Falcon* to the myriad of weird yet believable creatures that filled the screen in the cantina scene – Wookiees and Jawas and all of the far-out species in between.

The drawings and paintings that first helped George Lucas bring his vision to life fill the pages of this new retelling. Created by talented and now-legendary artists, this artwork helped everyone working on the film understand what was ahead. It illustrates the creativity that went into the film that not only led me toward a life of art and design, but that captivated the world. I hope this art inspires you the way it inspired me. May the Force be with you.

Troy Alders
Art Director, Lucasfilm

It was a time of war. The evil Galactic Empire ruled with an iron fist. Legions of armoured stormtroopers had seized planet after planet, crushing any sign of resistance, and their stranglehold on the galaxy seemed complete.

But just when things seemed darkest, hope was suddenly rekindled. Under the command of a Rebel Alliance, a fleet of ships attacked the heavily defended Imperial world of Scarif. Their objective was simple: to steal the blueprints to the Empire's terrible new weapon, the Death Star – a monstrous space station with the firepower to wipe out an entire planet.

The Rebels' triumph was short-lived. The plans to the Death Star were smuggled away on a blockade runner named the *Tantive IV*, but the Empire were right behind them. It wasn't long before the Rebel ship was hunted down and captured by an Imperial Star Destroyer, in the skies above the remote desert world of Tatooine.

Storyboard image of an Imperial Star Destroyer near Tatooine. **ALEX TAVOULARIS**

In the *Tantive IV*'s main corridor, Rebel troops gripped their blasters as they waited for Imperial soldiers to board the ship. Two droids were making their way along the passageway. 'They shut down the main reactor,' said the taller of the two robots, a golden protocol droid named C-3PO. 'We'll be destroyed for sure.'

His companion let out a beep of agreement. His name was R2-D2 and he was an astromech droid: short and dome-headed, with three legs and a single glowing eye.

Sparks began to fly, and the door at the end of the corridor exploded. Masked Imperial stormtroopers flooded through the opening. The Rebels returned fire but the stormtroopers were too many. The Rebels were forced to retreat.

Through the wrecked doorway strode a tall, terrifying figure.

The Alderaanian blockade runner *Tantive IV*. **JOE JOHNSTON**

Bounty hunter / dark knight
costume concept.
RALPH MCQUARRIE

He was dressed all in black, from his gleaming metallic helmet down to his flowing cloak and boots. Saying nothing, Darth Vader – the Empire's most feared agent – looked down at the motionless bodies littering the corridor. Then he strode away, with a platoon of stormtroopers hurrying behind.

In another part of the ship, C-3PO was searching for his counterpart, R2-D2. He found the little droid in a quiet corridor, but he wasn't alone. A young woman bent over him, dressed all in white. She inserted a datacard into Artoo's memory bank ... then vanished into the shadows.

The *Tantive IV* was now under the control of Darth Vader and his Imperial foot soldiers. The Dark Lord took the ship's captain by the throat, demanding that he reveal the location of the secret plans. But Captain Antilles refused to tell Vader anything.

As the captain's body crashed to the floor, Vader turned furiously to his troops. 'Tear this ship apart until you've found those plans,' he demanded. 'And bring me the passengers. I want them alive!'

Meanwhile, C-3PO had followed R2-D2 into the *Tantive IV*'s escape pod bay. To Threepio's dismay, the little astromech seemed determined to enter one of the pods. 'You're not permitted in there!' the golden droid protested.

But when blaster fire rocked the corridor, C-3PO knew he had no choice. 'I'm going to regret this,' he muttered as he climbed inside. The door slid shut and the escape pod launched into space.

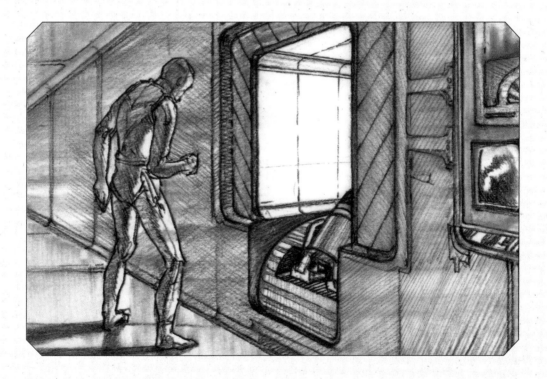

Storyboard image of C-3PO and R2-D2 entering an escape pod. **ALEX TAVOULARIS**

Storyboard / concept art of the escape pod heading down to Tatooine. JOE JOHNSTON

Aboard the Imperial Star Destroyer, two soldiers watched as the pod spiralled down towards the planet. But when one of them went to shoot it down, the other stayed his hand. 'Hold your fire. There are no life forms.'

On the Rebel ship, a platoon of stormtroopers had brought a valuable prisoner before Darth Vader. Her name was Princess Leia Organa, and she was one of the few people in the galaxy who wasn't afraid of the Dark Lord. 'I'm a member of the Imperial Senate on a diplomatic mission to Alderaan,' she told him angrily.

'You are part of the Rebel Alliance, and a traitor!' Darth Vader retorted.

An Imperial officer reported to Vader that the search had been completed, and the stolen plans were not aboard the ship. 'An escape pod was jettisoned during the fighting,' he admitted. 'But no life forms were aboard.'

Storyboard / concept art of C-3PO and R2-D2 in the escape pod, looking back at the Star Destroyer. **JOE JOHNSTON**

'She must have hidden the plans in the escape pod,' Darth Vader realised. 'Send a detachment down to retrieve them. See to it personally, Commander. There will be no one to stop us this time!'

Down on the desert world of Tatooine, C-3PO and R2-D2 had abandoned their escape pod and were making their way slowly through the dunes. 'What a desolate place this is,' moaned Threepio.

Artoo let out a whistle. He wanted to head towards a line of rocky hills, but C-3PO refused. 'Where do you think you're going? Well I'm not going that way. It's much too rocky. This way is much easier. What makes you think there are settlements over there?' Artoo let out a string of bleeps. 'What mission?' Threepio asked. 'Go that way. You'll be malfunctioning within a day, you nearsighted scrap pile.' And he strode off, leaving Artoo behind.

C-3PO wandered away, complaining bitterly. He passed the giant skeleton of a krayt dragon that lay bleached on the sand. Then he spotted something in the distance.

'A transport,' he said excitedly, waving his metal arms in the air. 'I'm saved! Over here. Hey! Hey! Please help!'

Meanwhile, R2-D2 had reached the dark hills. The little astromech whistled softly as he trundled through a stony ravine. Little did he know that he was being watched. Behind the rocks, hooded creatures known as Jawas whispered to one another. Their yellow eyes glowed as the droid passed by.

Then one of the Jawas sprang up in front of Artoo and fired an ion blaster. The blue energy bolt struck the droid, knocking him off his feet.

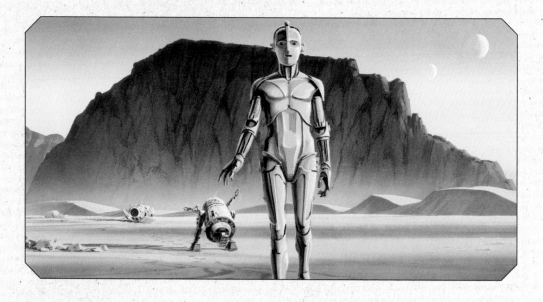

Concept art of C-3PO and R2-D2 on the planet of Tatooine after landing in the escape pod.
Ralph McQuarrie

The Jawa gestured eagerly. *'Utinni!'* he cried, and the others crowded round, lifting Artoo. They carried him through the ravine to their gigantic sandcrawler, where they fitted the little droid with a restraining bolt to prevent him from escaping. Then a large air-pipe snaked down from the sandcrawler and sucked Artoo inside.

Artoo was dumped into a large chamber filled with strange droids. They came in all shapes and sizes, from boxy power droids also known as gonk droids, to machines built for moisture farming, mining and security. Then a pair of glowing eyes spotted Artoo.

Storyboard / concept art of Jawas abducting R2-D2 and returning to their sandcrawler.
JOE JOHNSTON

'R2-D2, it is you!' C-3PO cried, as the sandcrawler shook and rumbled around them.

Elsewhere in the desert, Vader's stormtroopers had found the escape pod empty. One of the troopers discovered a small fragment of metal lying in the sand. 'Look, sir!' he exclaimed. 'Droids!'

Later that morning, the sandcrawler arrived at a small farmstead deep in the desert. The Jawas herded the droids down the ramp and lined them up for inspection.

From the domed settlement, two humans emerged. Owen Lars was older, with a weather-worn face and dusty brown robes. His nephew Luke Skywalker was a fresh-faced young man with tousled blond hair and a utility belt bristling with tools.

Owen studied the droids, selecting a red astromech named R5-D4. Then he walked over to C-3PO. 'Do you speak Bocce?' he asked.

'It's like a second language to me,' Threepio assured him.

'We'll take this one,' Owen told the Jawas. He beckoned to Luke. 'Take these two into the garage. I want them cleaned up before dinner.'

Luke's face fell. 'But I was going into Tosche Station to pick up some power converters!' With a sigh, he motioned C-3PO and R5-D4 to follow him. Threepio looked back regretfully as R2-D2 was left behind with the Jawas.

There was a sudden bang, and smoke began to gush from R5-D4's dome. Luke hurried over to take a look. 'This R2 unit has a bad motivator!'

Costume concept for Owen and Beru Lars. RALPH MCQUARRIE

Uncle Owen scowled. He was sure the Jawas were trying to cheat him. 'Excuse me, sir,' C-3PO said. 'But that R2 unit is in prime condition. A real bargain.' He pointed at R2-D2.

Owen turned to the Jawas. 'We'll take that one.' Artoo beeped happily as he was reunited with C-3PO.

In the farmstead's garage, Luke filled an oil bath for C-3PO. But the young man was in a sour mood. Recently, his friends Biggs and Tank had left for the Imperial Academy. Luke wanted to go too, but his uncle wouldn't let him.

'Biggs is right,' he complained. 'I'm never going to get out of here.' He grabbed a cleaning tool and went to work on R2-D2, scrubbing the dirt from the little droid's dome. 'It looks like you boys have seen a lot of action,' he observed.

C-3PO emerged from his oil bath. 'With all we've been through, sometimes I'm amazed we're in as good condition as we are. What with the Rebellion and all.'

Luke jumped up. 'You know of the Rebellion against the Empire? Have you been in many battles?'

'Several, I think,' Threepio said. 'Actually, there's not much to tell. I'm not much more than an interpreter and I'm not very good at telling stories. Well, not at making them interesting anyway.'

Luke returned to Artoo, prying at a fragment of metal that had become jammed in the astromech's neck joint. 'Well, my little friend, you've got something jammed in here real good. Were you on a cruiser, or...'

Luke's pick suddenly snapped – and a beam of blue light sprang from the little droid's dome. It was a hologram, in the form of Princess Leia.

'Help me, Obi-Wan Kenobi,' the Princess pleaded. 'You're my only hope.' Then the hologram flickered, and the message repeated.

Luke stared in amazement. 'She's beautiful,' he gaped. 'Is there any more to this recording?'

Artoo gave a beep, and C-3PO translated. 'He says he is the property of Obi-Wan Kenobi, a resident of these parts, and it's a private message for him. Frankly, I don't know what he's talking about.'

'I wonder if he means old Ben Kenobi,' Luke mused. 'He lives out beyond the Dune Sea. He's kind of a strange old hermit.'

Artoo gave another beep. 'He says the restraining bolt has short circuited his recording system. He suggests that if you remove the bolt, he might be able to play back the entire recording.'

Luke crouched and removed the bolt, but just then a voice called his name. 'I'll be right back,' he said, and hurried away.

Costume concept for Luke Skywalker.
RALPH MCQUARRIE

Inside the sunken farmstead, Luke's Aunt Beru was serving dinner. While they ate, Luke told his uncle what Artoo had said about Obi-Wan Kenobi. 'I thought he might have meant old Ben. Do you know what he's talking about? I wonder if he's related to Ben.'

Uncle Owen shook his head. 'That wizard's just a crazy old man.' He told

Concept art for Luke Skywalker and the droids in the deserts of Tatooine, with Mos Eisley in the distance. RALPH MCQUARRIE

Luke to have Artoo's memory erased. 'That'll be the end of it. It belongs to us now.'

'But what if this Obi-Wan comes looking for him?' Luke asked.

'He won't,' Owen said firmly. 'I don't think he exists any more. He died about the same time as your father.'

Luke looked up. 'He knew my father?'

Owen glowered. 'I told you to forget it.'

Luke stared down at his dinner. 'I think those new droids are going to work out fine,' he said. With the droids to help, he thought it was time for him to apply to the academy instead of staying on the farm another season.

Uncle Owen sighed. 'This year we'll make enough on the harvest that I'll be able to hire some more hands and then you can go to the academy next year. You must understand I need you here, Luke.'

Luke stumbled to his feet, leaving his supper half-eaten. After he was gone, Beru turned sadly to her husband. 'He can't stay here forever.' Owen promised he'd make it up to him, but Beru objected. 'Luke's just not a farmer. He has too much of his father in him.'

Owen Lars frowned. 'That's what I'm afraid of.'

Outside the farmstead, Luke gazed towards the twin suns of Tatooine as they sank towards the horizon. He felt trapped and hopeless. Deep inside, he knew that he was meant for more than a farmer's life.

But when he returned to the garage, he found C-3PO alone. Artoo had run away. Luke cursed, hurrying outside and scanning the horizon with a pair of macrobinoculars. There was no sign of the little droid and they couldn't go after him.

'It's too dangerous with all the Sand People around,' he told Threepio. 'We'll have to wait until morning. You know, that little droid is going to cause me a lot of trouble.'

C-3PO nodded sympathetically. 'Oh, he excels at that, sir.'

At dawn, they set out to find Artoo. Threepio piloted Luke's landspeeder, floating swiftly over the sandy terrain. It wasn't long before they picked up a signal on the scanner.

But when they caught up with R2-D2, the little droid began to beep fearfully. 'He says there are several creatures approaching from the southeast,' C-3PO warned Luke.

The young man grabbed his rifle. 'Sand People. Or worse. Come on, let's go have a look.'

Concept art of a Tusken Raider (detail). RALPH McQUARRIE

Concept art of a Tusken Raider. **RALPH MCQUARRIE**

From a high ridge, Luke spotted a pair of shaggy creatures called banthas waiting below. But as Luke peered through his macrobinoculars, a terrifying figure reared up right in front of him!

It was a Tusken Raider, one of the tribes of desert-dwellers known to the locals as Sand People. Another raider had sneaked behind them, and as C-3PO toppled over in shock, he drove Luke to the ground with his spiked gaffi stick, cackling coarsely.

Down in the canyon, R2-D2 waited silently. He saw the Sand People carrying Luke's unconscious body back to the landspeeder and ransacking the vehicle.

Suddenly, a fearful howl echoed from the canyon walls. The Sand People looked up as a dark figure appeared, letting out another terrible cry. The Tusken Raiders fled, leaving Luke lying on the sand.

The robed figure hurried to the boy's side. Artoo gave a frightened beep and the figure looked up, throwing back his hood. It was an elderly man with a white beard and a kindly face. 'Hello there,' the man said.

Luke groaned. 'Ben Kenobi? Boy, am I glad to see you.' Wincing, he sat up.

'Tell me, young Luke, what brings you out this far?' asked Ben.

'This little droid,' he said, gesturing to Artoo. 'He claims to be the property of an Obi-Wan Kenobi. Is he a relative of yours?'

The old man seemed surprised.

Concept art of Obi-Wan Kenobi.
RALPH MCQUARRIE

'Obi-Wan? Now that's a name I've not heard in a long time.'

'I think my uncle knows him,' Luke went on. 'He said he was dead.'

The old man smiled. 'Oh, he's not dead. Not yet.'

'You know him?' Luke asked.

'Of course I know him. He's me. I haven't gone by the name of Obi-Wan since before you were born.' He helped Luke to his feet. 'I think we better get indoors. The Sand People are easily startled, but they'll soon be back and in greater numbers.'

He took Luke and the droids back to his home, a stone hut deep in the desert, where Luke asked Obi-Wan about his father. Uncle Owen had always told Luke that his father was a navigator on a spice freighter. But now, Obi-Wan revealed that he had been a member of the Jedi, guardians of peace and justice in the time of the Old Republic.

He took something from a wooden chest. 'Your father's lightsaber,' he told Luke, handing the young man a small metal cylinder. 'This is the weapon of a Jedi Knight.'

Costume concept for Princess Leia. RALPH MCQUARRIE

Costume concept for Darth Vader.
RALPH McQUARRIE

Luke touched a button and the laser sword sprang into life. Its blue blade sliced through the air, humming with power. 'How did my father die?' he asked Obi-Wan.

'A young Jedi named Darth Vader, who was a pupil of mine until he turned to evil, helped the Empire hunt down and destroy the Jedi Knights. He betrayed and murdered your father. Now the Jedi are all but extinct,' Obi-Wan explained. 'Vader was seduced by the dark side of the Force. The Force is what gives a Jedi his power. It's an energy field created by all living things.'

Now they were finally able to view the entire message that Princess Leia had hidden inside Artoo's memory banks. She pleaded for Obi-Wan to bring the droid to her home planet of Alderaan, and deliver the Death Star plans to the Rebel Alliance.

Obi-Wan listened thoughtfully, then said, 'You must learn the ways of the Force, if you're to come with me to Alderaan.'

Luke got to his feet. 'I'm not going to Alderaan,' he said firmly. 'I'm going home.'

Obi-Wan frowned. 'You must do what you feel is right, of course.'

Meanwhile, Darth Vader had returned to the Empire's dreadful new battle station, the Death Star. Accompanied by the station's commander, a cruel, grey-faced man named Grand Moff Tarkin, the Dark Lord entered the conference room to find a group of high-ranking Imperial officers arguing amongst themselves.

Concept art for the interrogator droid on the Death Star. RALPH MCQUARRIE

Some warned that the Rebel Alliance were now a serious threat, while others argued that they were no match for the Death Star.

But when one officer spoke rashly to Lord Vader, the Dark Lord made a demonstration of his power. An invisible hand seemed to tighten around the officer's throat, and he began to splutter and choke.

At Tarkin's command, Lord Vader released the officer. 'This bickering is pointless,' Tarkin snapped. 'Lord Vader will provide us with the location of the Rebel fortress by the time this station is operational. We will then crush the Rebellion with one swift stroke.'

But there was only one person on the Death Star who knew the location of the Rebels' secret base. Princess Leia shivered in her prison cell as Vader entered, accompanied by a gleaming black interrogator droid. The

Storyboard image of Luke and his new friends entering Mos Eisley spaceport. JOE JOHNSTON

Dark Lord was determined to use any means necessary to make her tell him where the Rebels were hiding.

Back on Tatooine, Luke and the others had made a shocking discovery. The Jawas' sandcrawler had been attacked, and Obi-Wan was certain that Imperial stormtroopers were responsible.

Luke's face fell. He knew the troopers must be hunting for R2-D2, and that the Jawas would have told them who they sold the droid to. Ignoring Obi-Wan's warning, he leapt into his landspeeder and fired up the engines.

But it was too late. As he approached the Lars farmstead, Luke saw a pillar of smoke churning into the sky. As he stumbled from the speeder, he cried out the names of his aunt and uncle. But they were gone – murdered by the Empire. Luke hung his head in despair.

Filled with grief, Luke returned to the sandcrawler. 'I want to come with you to Alderaan,' he told Obi-Wan. 'There's nothing for me here now. I want to learn the ways of the Force and become a Jedi, like my father.'

The old man nodded, and took Luke's arm in sympathy.

First, they travelled to the nearest spaceport: Mos Eisley, a notorious hotbed of criminal activity. But as the speeder floated through the bustling, sandy streets, they were stopped by a stormtrooper patrol.

Luke tried to keep calm as their captain demanded to see his identification. But Obi-Wan just waved a hand. 'You don't need to see his identification,' he said in a gentle, persuasive voice. 'These aren't the droids you're looking for.'

'We don't need to see his identification,' the stormtrooper repeated. 'These aren't the droids we're looking for.' Then he waved the landspeeder away. 'Move along.'

When they were safely out of sight, Luke turned to Obi-Wan in amazement. He didn't understand why the stormtroopers had let them go. 'The Force can have a strong influence on the weak-minded,' the old man chuckled.

Next, they needed to find a pilot willing to fly them to Alderaan. Obi-Wan knew that the best place to look would be Chalmun's Cantina, a smoky, low-ceilinged bar populated by smugglers, bounty hunters and aliens of every imaginable species.

Luke saw a hammer-headed Ithorian and a furry Talz; a snake-like Lamproid and a crafty, horned Devaronian. On the stage, a band of dome-headed Bith were playing an upbeat tune to the delight of the crowd.

But as they headed for the bar, the owner gestured angrily at C-3PO and R2-D2. 'We don't serve their kind here,' he growled. 'They'll have to wait outside.'

Luke sipped his drink and tried to blend in. Then he felt a hand on his shoulder. A fierce Aqualish growled in his native language. 'He doesn't like you,' the creature's human companion translated. 'I don't like you either. You just watch yourself.'

Luke turned away, but the pair were determined to make trouble. When Obi-Wan Kenobi tried to reason with them, they shoved Luke aside and reached for their blasters. Then there was a sudden flash of blue light, followed by a howl of pain.

Early concept art of Luke duelling an alien in the Mos Eisley cantina. **RALPH MCQUARRIE**

The Aqualish's arm lay on the floor in a pool of blood. Obi-Wan deactivated his lightsaber and returned it to his belt. Then he bent to help Luke to his feet.

'Chewbacca here is first mate on a ship that might suit us,' he said, gesturing to a tall figure standing at his side. It was a towering, shaggy-haired creature called a Wookiee, with bright black eyes and a silver bandolier.

Chewbacca led them to a table in the shadows and introduced them to his captain, Han Solo, a brash Corellian smuggler. Solo agreed to fly them to Alderaan – at the cost of ten thousand Imperial credits.

Luke was outraged, but Obi-Wan knew they had no choice. 'We can pay you two thousand now,' he told Solo, 'plus another fifteen when we reach Alderaan.'

Solo considered it. 'Okay, you guys got yourselves a ship. We'll leave as soon as you're ready. Docking Bay Ninety-Four.'

Costume concept for Han Solo. RALPH McQUARRIE

Chewbacca headed off to get the ship ready, leaving Han Solo to finish his drink. But as he was preparing to exit the cantina, Solo felt the muzzle of a blaster poking him in the chest.

A Rodian bounty hunter named Greedo forced Solo back into his seat. The smuggler owed a lot of money to Greedo's boss, the notorious gangster Jabba the Hutt. Greedo was determined to collect it – alive or dead.

Han Solo was too quick for him. Two shots rang out, and the Rodian collapsed face-down on the table. Solo apologised to the bartender and left the Cantina.

But when he reached Docking Bay 94, Solo found Jabba himself waiting for him. The slug-like crime lord turned as Solo approached. His patience was wearing thin, and he wanted what Solo owed him – and no more excuses.

Storyboard for the Special Edition scene in which Han Solo confronts Jabba the Hutt.
GEORGE HULL

Han assured Jabba that he'd get his money, along with an extra fifteen per cent on top. Jabba wasn't happy, but he knew that Han was the best smuggler in the galaxy.

Luke Skywalker, Obi-Wan Kenobi and the two droids moved through the teeming streets of Mos Eisley, heading for Docking Bay 94. But they were not alone: a long-snouted Garindan followed, reporting their location to the Imperial authorities.

Luke wasn't impressed when he first laid eyes on Han Solo's ship, the *Millennium Falcon*. 'What a piece of junk!' he hooted.

In the cockpit, Chewbacca was preparing for take-off. But before he could start the engines, a platoon of Imperial stormtroopers burst into the docking bay.

'Stop that ship! Blast 'em!' the lead trooper shouted, as laser bolts ricocheted from the walls of the hangar.

Han Solo sprinted onto the *Millennium Falcon* as blasters sizzled the air. 'Chewie, get us out of here!' he yelled, and the ship's main engines roared into life. The stormtroopers could only watch as the *Falcon* blasted free of Tatooine's gravity, heading for deep space.

But their troubles weren't over. As Han Solo hurried to program the ship's computer for light speed, three Imperial Star Destroyers were moving to cut off their escape. Solo ordered his passengers to strap in, then he reached for the *Falcon*'s controls. The distant stars turned to streaks of light as the ship blasted into hyperspace.

Concept art for the Death Star's superlaser tunnel. **RALPH MCQUARRIE**

Many light years away, the Death Star was approaching the peaceful planet of Alderaan. In the control room, Princess Leia had been brought before Governor Tarkin. She was angry and defiant – until Tarkin told her what was about to happen.

'I have chosen to test this station's destructive power on your home planet of Alderaan,' he said cruelly. The Princess pleaded for the lives of her people, but the Governor just sneered. 'You would prefer another target? A military target? Then name the system. I grow tired of asking this, so it will be the last time. Where is the Rebel base?'

Princess Leia gazed down at her home world, imagining the millions of lives under threat. 'Dantooine,' she said at last. 'They're on Dantooine.'

Tarkin smiled, then he turned to his officers. 'There. You see, Lord Vader, she can be reasonable. Continue with the operation. You may fire when ready.'

Revised concept for Chewbacca.
RALPH MCQUARRIE

Princess Leia cried out in horror, but there was nothing she could do. Darth Vader gripped her shoulder as the Death Star's superlaser hummed into life. Beams of light erupted from the emitter, joining to form a single bolt of ultra-destructive power. It struck the planet Alderaan and blasted the entire world to pieces.

In the main hold of the *Millennium Falcon*, Obi-Wan Kenobi clutched his chest and sank into a chair. 'I felt a great disturbance in the Force,' he told Luke. 'As if millions of voices suddenly cried out in terror and were suddenly silenced. I fear something terrible has happened.'

Nearby, R2-D2 was playing a game called Dejarik against the Wookiee, Chewbacca. On a chequered table, strange holographic creatures battled one another. But when Artoo began to win, Chewbacca let out a howl.

'Let him have it. It's not wise to upset a Wookiee,' Han Solo warned.

'But sir,' C-3PO said, 'nobody worries about upsetting a droid.'

'That's 'cause a droid don't pull people's arms out of their sockets when they lose. Wookiees are known to do that.'

C-3PO nodded. 'I see your point, sir. I suggest a new strategy, Artoo. Let the Wookiee win.'

Luke was learning how to use his father's lightsaber, practising his fighting skills against a sphere-shaped remote. He tried to feel the Force flowing through him, just as Obi-Wan had instructed.

But when a blast from the remote struck Luke in a tender spot, Han Solo laughed aloud. He had seen a lot in his travels across the galaxy, but he didn't believe in the Force. 'It's all a lot of simple tricks and nonsense,' he said.

Obi-Wan suggested that Luke try again – but this time wearing a helmet that restricted his vision. 'With the blast shield down, I can't even see!' Luke protested. 'How am I supposed to fight?'

'Your eyes can deceive you. Don't trust them. Stretch out with your feelings,' Obi-Wan told him.

This time, when the remote fired, Luke moved instinctively to block the blast. 'You see? You can do it,' Obi-Wan congratulated him. 'You've taken your first step into a larger world.'

But as the *Millennium Falcon* approached the Alderaan system, it was clear that something was very wrong. There was no sign of the planet, just a shower of floating asteroids. Obi-Wan realised at once what had happened.

'Destroyed,' he told the others. 'By the Empire.'

Luke couldn't believe that such a thing was possible, but there was no time to discuss it. A ship had appeared on their scopes: a small Imperial TIE fighter. It blasted the *Falcon*, then it streaked away.

'He's heading for that small moon,' Luke pointed.

'That's no moon,' Obi-Wan told him. 'It's a space station.' Han Solo tried to turn the *Falcon* around, but it was too late. They were caught in an invisible tractor beam, pulling them steadily closer to the Death Star.

Concept art for the Death Star docking bay where the *Falcon* has landed. RALPH MCQUARRIE

On the battle station, Grand Moff Tarkin received a report that a ship had been captured. 'They must be trying to return the stolen plans to the Princess. She may yet be of some use to us,' Darth Vader said, and went to investigate.

But when his men searched the ship, they found no sign of anyone on board. 'According to the log, the crew abandoned ship right after take-off,' the commander reported. 'It must be a decoy. Several of the escape pods have been jettisoned.'

'Send a scanning crew aboard,' Vader ordered. 'I want every part of this

ship checked. I sense something... a presence I've not felt since...'

On the *Falcon*, Han Solo had hidden with his passengers inside a secret smuggling compartment. He and Luke lured a pair of stormtroopers on board, then blasted them and stole their uniforms.

The officers on duty in a nearby control room noticed the missing guards, but before they could investigate further, an angry Wookiee came roaring into the room! Chewbacca smashed one officer aside, Han blasted the other, and Luke, Ben and the droids hurried inside.

R2-D2 plugged himself into the Death Star's computer network. It wasn't

Concept art for the Death Star interior, featuring Chewbacca and a disguised Han and Luke.
RALPH MCQUARRIE

long before he had located the reactor that powered the tractor beam.

'I don't think you boys can help. I must go alone,' Obi-Wan told the others. 'Be patient. Luke, stay and watch over the droids. They must be delivered safely or other star systems will suffer the same fate as Alderaan. Your destiny lies along a different path from mine. The Force will be with you, always.' Then he strode from the room.

Suddenly, R2-D2 let out an urgent beep. 'He says "I've found her" and keeps repeating "she's here,"' C-3PO translated. 'Level five. Detention block A A-twenty-three. I'm afraid she's scheduled to be terminated.'

Artoo had found the location of Princess Leia! Han was confused until Luke explained that Leia was a rebel princess who was in trouble. 'We've got to do something!' he said.

But Han Solo refused to leave the safety of the control room. 'I'm not going anywhere.'

'She's rich,' Luke told him. 'Rich, powerful. If you were to rescue her, the reward would be more wealth than you can imagine.'

Solo frowned. 'I can imagine quite a bit.' But he grudgingly agreed to help the Princess.

Donning their stormtrooper disguises, Luke and Han placed Chewbacca in binders to make it appear that he was their prisoner. Leaving Artoo and Threepio in the control room, they took an elevator to the Death Star's detention block.

A prison officer looked up as they entered. He stared at Chewbacca in disgust. 'Where are you taking this... thing?'

The Wookiee gave a roar and flung his arms in the air. 'Look out! He's loose!' Han cried, and pulled out his blaster.

Everything was chaos. As the prison officers ran to restrain Chewbacca, Luke and Han fired wildly at everything in sight. Cameras exploded on the walls, and Imperial troops were blasted off their feet.

As the smoke cleared, Luke ran to find the Princess while Han attempted to prevent any more stormtroopers from coming to investigate. When his efforts to persuade them proved fruitless, he simply blasted the comlink.

'Luke!' he shouted. 'We're going to have company!'

Costume concept art for Imperial soldiers.
RALPH McQUARRIE

Princess Leia looked up as the door to her cell slid open. She frowned as Luke entered. 'Aren't you a little short for a stormtrooper?'

Luke removed his helmet. 'I'm Luke Skywalker. I'm here to rescue you. I've got your R2 unit. I'm here with Ben Kenobi.' Together, they ran from the cell.

Sensing that Obi-Wan Kenobi was aboard the Death Star, Darth Vader went to warn Governor Tarkin. But the commander wasn't convinced. 'The Jedi are extinct,' Tarkin insisted. 'Their fire has gone out of the universe.'

When his officers reported a disturbance in the prison, however, Vader's suspicions were confirmed. 'Obi-Wan is here. The Force is with him.'

Tarkin said that the old Jedi must not be allowed to escape. 'Escape is not his plan,' the Dark Lord replied. 'I must face him alone.'

In the detention block, Luke and the others were backed into a corridor with only one exit. 'This is some rescue. When you came in here, didn't you have a plan for getting out?' the Princess asked.

'Hey, he's the brains,' Han retorted, pointing at Luke. As stormtroopers blasted them relentlessly, Princess Leia grabbed Luke's weapon and blew open an access panel in the wall.

'Into the garbage chute, flyboy!' she snapped at Han Solo, and leapt through the opening, followed by Chewbacca.

Costume concept art for Princess Leia. **RALPH MCQUARRIE**

Han looked at Luke and raised an eyebrow, then let out a whoop and dove into the shaft.

Han splashed down into a pool of filth. They were in a garbage container filled with broken machine parts and noxious liquid. But when Han tried to blast the magnetically sealed door, his laser bolt ricocheted dangerously off the walls.

'Put that thing away!' Princess Leia ordered. 'You're going to get us all killed!'

Suddenly, there was a deep groan from below. 'There's something alive in here,' Luke said nervously. He didn't notice the single, inhuman eye rising from the water and watching him. Without warning, a tentacle snaked from the water and wrapped around his leg. Han fired into the water, but the tentacle dragged Luke down. An awful silence fell.

A loud, metallic creak came suddenly from inside the walls. Moments later, Luke splashed to the surface. 'It just let go of me and disappeared,' he spluttered.

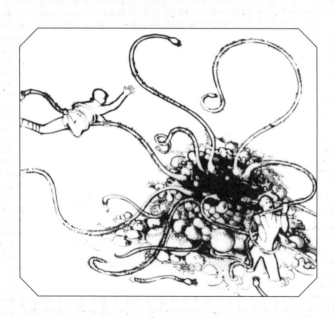

Concept art for the dianoga. JOHN BARRY

The creak came again, and now they realised what was happening. The creature had fled because the walls were moving inwards. Before long they would be crushed, along with all the Imperial garbage.

'Try and brace it with something!' Leia cried, but it was no use. Chewbacca let out a howl of despair.

Then Luke remembered. 'Threepio!' he yelled into his comlink. 'Threepio?' There was no answer.

C-3PO had deactivated his communicator when he and R2-D2 were forced out of hiding by an Imperial patrol. Thinking fast, C-3PO pretended to be on their side. 'They're madmen! They're heading for the prison level. If you hurry, you might catch them!'

After outwitting the troopers, they returned to the hangar that housed the *Millennium Falcon*. But Luke and the others weren't there.

'See if they've been captured,' C-3PO urged R2-D2. 'Hurry!'

Concept art for R2-D2 / astromech droids.
RALPH MCQUARRIE

As Artoo scanned the Imperial network, he beeped at Threepio. The tall droid looked shocked. 'The comlink. I turned it off!'

He activated his communicator just as Luke and the others were about to be crushed by the enclosing walls. 'Listen to me!' Luke yelled. 'Shut down all the garbage mashers on the detention level!'

Threepio passed the message to Artoo, and just in the nick of time! Luke whooped with relief as the walls ground to a halt. The two droids had saved them.

Elsewhere on the Death Star, Obi-Wan Kenobi had located the power source for the station's tractor beam. Balanced high above an impossibly deep ventilation shaft, the old man deactivated the reactor. He used the Force to make a noise which distracted the stormtroopers on duty, then he slipped silently past them, and was gone.

As Luke and the others raced back towards the *Falcon*, Princess Leia turned to Han Solo. 'I don't know who you are or where you came from, but from now on, you do as I tell you, okay?'

Han's jaw dropped. 'Look, Your Worshipfulness. Let's get one thing straight. I take orders from just one person – me.'

The Princess rolled her eyes. 'It's a wonder you're still alive.' Their bickering was interrupted by the sudden arrival of a stormtrooper patrol. With a yell, Han charged at the troopers, with Chewbacca on his heels. But as they hurtled around a corner they found an entire platoon waiting for them. Han turned and fled, firing over his shoulder as the stormtroopers gave chase.

Luke and Leia had run in the opposite direction, pursued by a second patrol. As they burst through an open doorway, Luke skidded to a halt. Ahead of them was a yawning chasm, much too wide to jump across. As the chasing stormtroopers fired at them, Leia hit the controls to close the door they had come through, and Luke blasted them to pieces.

Now they were trapped. But as more troopers appeared above them, Luke reached for his utility belt and drew out a steel cable attached to a grappling hook. Swinging the cable, he managed to hook it to a beam high above them. Leia fired her blaster, sending one of the troopers tumbling down into the abyss.

Storyboard image of Luke and Leia trapped by a dead end on the Death Star. **JOE JOHNSTON**

Then Luke took hold of the Princess. Leaning closer, Leia kissed him on the cheek. 'For luck,' she said then Luke leapt, swinging them both across the chasm.

Obi-Wan Kenobi slipped through the corridors of the Death Star, drawing closer to the *Millennium Falcon*. But before he could reach it, he came face to face with an old acquaintance. Darth Vader stood blocking his path, a red lightsaber humming in his hand.

'I've been waiting for you, Obi-Wan,' the Dark Lord boomed. 'We meet again at last. The circle is now complete. When I left you, I was but the learner. Now I am the master.'

Concept art for Darth Vader. **Ralph McQuarrie**

'Only a master of evil, Darth,' Obi-Wan replied.

Vader strode forward, raising his blade. Obi-Wan took a step back and ignited his saber. Vader swung and the laser swords clashed together, filling the hallway with light and noise. 'Your powers are weak, old man,' he said.

Obi Wan moved swiftly, countering blow after blow. 'You can't win, Darth,' he told his former apprentice. 'If you strike me down, I will become more powerful than you can possibly imagine.'

'You should not have come back,' Vader replied, lunging at Obi-Wan, but the old Jedi was too quick.

Spotting the duel from across the hangar, the stormtroopers guarding the *Millennium Falcon* peeled away, running to the aid of their overlord.

Costume concept for Obi-Wan Kenobi. **RALPH MCQUARRIE**

Luke, Leia, Han and Chewie had made it back to the hangar, where Artoo and Threepio joined them. With the guards distracted, they ran for the *Falcon*. But as he neared the *Falcon*, Luke saw his master locked in combat with the monstrous Darth Vader.

Storyboard image showing Luke, Leia and Chewbacca on the *Millennium Falcon*'s entry ramp.
IVOR BEDDOES

Obi-Wan glanced up and saw Luke. For a moment, their eyes met. Then Kenobi smiled. He knew what he had to do.

Raising his lightsaber, Obi-Wan left himself wide open to Darth Vader's next attack. The Dark Lord swung his saber, but as the killing blow landed, the old Jedi seemed to ... vanish.

Luke cried out and the stormtroopers turned. Darth Vader strode to the place where Obi-Wan had fallen, but all he found were an empty cloak and the hilt of Kenobi's lightsaber.

Luke was consumed with fury, blasting the stormtroopers and ignoring Leia's call to get back to the ship. Then a disembodied voice echoed out of nowhere.

'Run, Luke, run!' Obi-Wan commanded. Luke knew he had no choice.

Aboard the *Falcon*, Chewbacca hit the throttle and the ship thundered out of the Death Star's hangar. In the hold, Luke was full of grief. He couldn't believe that they'd lost Obi-Wan Kenobi. But when Han Solo came to warn him that they were not yet out of danger, Luke sprang into action. Four Imperial TIE fighters were closing in...

Luke and Han each took control of one of the *Falcon*'s laser cannons as the enemy fighters came screaming towards them. Fires broke out as energy bolts rocked the ship.

Han was the first to shoot down one of the attacking fighters, followed swiftly by Luke. The last two fighters turned to attack, and Han grinned as Luke took out another fighter. Soon the final TIE fighter erupted in a ball of gas and flame, and the *Millennium Falcon* was free.

Back on the Death Star, Grand Moff Tarkin faced Darth Vader. 'You're sure the homing beacon is secure aboard their ship?' he asked. 'I'm taking an awful risk, Vader. This had better work.' Vader assured him that it would.

But on the *Millennium Falcon*, Princess Leia wasn't fooled. 'They let us go,' she told Han. 'It's the only reason for the ease of our escape.' The Empire must be tracking the

Costume concept for Rebel Biggs Darklighter. RALPH MCQUARRIE

Falcon, she explained – but at least the Death Star plans were still safe in R2-D2's memory banks. 'It's not over yet,' she said.

The smuggler scowled. 'It is for me, sister. I expect to be well paid.'

Princess Leia looked at him coldly. 'If money is all that you love, then that's what you will receive.'

Soon they had arrived at the coordinates provided by Princess Leia. As they approached the jungle moon of Yavin 4, the *Falcon* was scanned by a Rebel trooper hidden high in the trees.

The Rebel base was hidden inside a huge stone structure called the Great Massassi Temple. As they were taken through the temple's main hangar, Luke saw ranks of Rebel fighter ships and hundreds of pilots, soldiers and ground crew.

Princess Leia handed R2-D2 to the Rebel authorities so that the information he contained could be studied. But they were running out of time. The Death Star had already entered the Yavin system and would soon come within firing range.

As howls echoed through the jungle outside, a Rebel leader named General Dodonna gathered his troops for a briefing. Luke, Han and Chewbacca listened in as he unveiled his plan for a sneak attack by a fleet of small fighters. The Death Star had enormous firepower, but its defences were designed for a large scale assault.

'An analysis of the plans provided by Princess Leia has demonstrated a weakness in the battle station,' Dodonna told them. The target was a small thermal exhaust port, only two metres wide, at the end of a trench on the Death Star's surface. A precise hit with photon torpedoes would start a chain reaction which should destroy the station.

Luke Skywalker had volunteered to join the attack. But as he and his fellow pilots headed for their ships, Luke discovered Han Solo preparing to leave.

'So, you've got your reward and you're just leaving, then?' he said bitterly.

Solo nodded. 'That's right, yeah! I got some old debts I've got to pay off with this stuff. Even if I didn't, you don't think I'd be fool enough to stick around here, do you? Why don't you come with us? You're pretty good in a fight. We could use you.'

But Luke turned him down. He was part of something bigger now.

'What's wrong?' Leia asked him, seeing him looking sad.

'Oh, it's Han! I don't know, I really thought he'd change his mind,' Luke told her.

'He's got to follow his own path,' Leia replied. 'No one can choose it for him.'

'I only wish Ben were here,' he said.

Concept art showing a Rebel sentry tower on Yavin 4.
RALPH McQUARRIE

Luke found another old friend installed in the back of his X-wing fighter: R2-D2. The little droid beeped a greeting as Luke hopped into the cockpit.

'Hang on tight, Artoo,' C-3PO told his counterpart. 'You've got to come back. You wouldn't want my life to get boring, would you?' R2-D2 gave a whistle, then it was time for take-off.

The hangar rang to the roar of engines as the Rebel pilots donned their helmets. As his ship rose into the air, Luke heard that disembodied voice again.

Storyboard image for Biggs Darklighter (with an all-seeing eye on his helmet) in his X-wing cockpit. **JOE JOHNSTON**

'Luke, the Force will be with you,' Obi-Wan told him. Luke gritted his teeth and prepared for battle.

The Rebel fleet soared away. The Death Star was just fifteen minutes from firing range. After that, the Rebel base would be utterly destroyed.

Concept art of a Death Star turbolaser battery.
Joe Johnston

Luke had been given the call sign Red Five, and as they approached the battle station he heard each of his fellow pilots reporting in. 'Look at the size of that thing,' marvelled Red Two, whose name was Wedge Antilles.

'Cut the chatter, Red Two. Accelerate to attack speed,' commanded Red Leader. 'This is it, boys.'

The fighters spiralled down towards the Death Star, heading for a narrow trench that housed the tiny exhaust port. Defensive cannons fired a volley of lasers as the ships approached. Down in the Rebel control room, Princess Leia and her fellow leaders listened fearfully as their pilots radioed back.

Outside the station, Rebel pilot Biggs Darklighter, an old friend of Luke's from Tatooine, was ready to try his first attack run. He ordered a pilot

A TIE fighter pursues an X-wing during the Death Star assault. **JOE JOHNSTON**

named Porkins to cover him. But a blast from one of the cannons struck Porkins's ship, tearing it apart. The Rebels had lost their first man.

Soon, Rebel scanners picked up enemy fighters heading their way. A squadron of TIE fighters screeched closer, obliterating one of the Rebel ships. But when an Imperial ship swooped in behind Biggs, Luke was there to save his friend. He fired, blowing the enemy fighter to pieces.

A group of Rebel Y-wings entered the trench, evading the enemy cannons as they headed for the exhaust port. As they approached their target, however, the guns suddenly fell silent. Three TIE fighters were moving to attack – and the lead ship was piloted by none other than Darth Vader.

'I'll take them myself,' the Dark Lord told his men. Luke could only watch as one after another, the Y-wings were shot down.

Poster concept art for the Death Star assault. JOHN BERKEY

In the Death Star's control room, an aide approached Grand Moff Tarkin, offering to ready his ship in case the Rebels were successful. 'Evacuate?' Tarkin asked disbelievingly. 'In our moment of triumph? I think you overestimate their chances.' He was sure that this ragtag army posed no threat to his battle station.

Meanwhile, Red Leader had guided another group of fighters into the trench. Vader was right behind them, taking out first one, then two of Red Leader's wingmen. But the Dark Lord was too late. Red Leader was in

Concept art for the Death Star trench run. **RALPH MCQUARRIE**

range. He fired, and his torpedoes streaked towards the target.

The shot was no good. The torpedoes missed, exploding on the surface of the Death Star. And as Red Leader turned to flee, Darth Vader's TIE fighter swooped in. Red Leader's X-wing slammed into the battle station and burst into flame.

Luke saw the ship explode and knew that time was running out. Flanked by Biggs and Wedge, he flew at full speed into the trench. But Darth Vader's fighter was right behind them and closing fast.

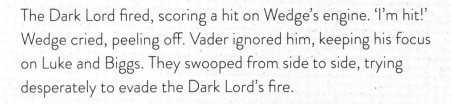

The Dark Lord fired, scoring a hit on Wedge's engine. 'I'm hit!' Wedge cried, peeling off. Vader ignored him, keeping his focus on Luke and Biggs. They swooped from side to side, trying desperately to evade the Dark Lord's fire.

It was no good. Biggs's ship was hit, and Luke watched as his best friend's ship exploded into shards of flame. There was no time to grieve. He knew that he was the Rebels' last hope for victory.

Luke switched on his targeting computer and prepared to fire his torpedoes. As he struggled to lock on to the target, Ben Kenobi's ghostly voice spoke to him once more. 'Use the Force, Luke,' the old Jedi told him. 'Let go. Luke, trust me.'

Luke deactivated his computer. He was determined to trust his instincts.

Poster concept art for the Death Star assault. JOHN BERKEY

Darth Vader fired again, and his laser bolt struck R2-D2, frying the little droid's circuits. Luke forced himself to stay focused, gripping the controls as he raced closer to the target.

The Death Star cleared the planet. The Rebel base was now in range. Grand Moff Tarkin gave the order to fire, and the battle station's superlaser began to hum.

Darth Vader had locked on to Luke's ship. 'I have you now,' he growled.

Then without warning a blast of laser fire came from above, sending the Dark Lord's ship spiralling into space. Han Solo let out a yell as the *Millennium Falcon* swooped overhead.

'You're all clear, kid!' he told Luke. 'Now let's blow this thing and go home.'

Luke fired his torpedoes, watching as they sped straight and true towards the target. They entered the tiny exhaust port and Luke peeled away, soaring back towards the *Falcon*.

In the Death Star's control room, Grand Moff Tarkin had no idea what was about to happen. Before the superlaser could fire, the chain reaction from Luke's direct hit tore the entire battle station to pieces in a vast explosion.

For a moment, the blackness of space was lit with countless shooting stars. The Empire's great weapon was no more.

As he leapt from the cockpit of his X-wing, Luke saw Leia and Han running towards him across the Rebel hangar. The three friends embraced warmly as all around them people whooped and cheered.

But when he saw R2-D2, Luke's face fell. The little droid's dome was blackened and scorched. 'You must repair him,' C-3PO pleaded.

Luke placed a hand on Threepio's arm. 'He'll be all right.'

Some time later, the soldiers of the Rebel Alliance gathered in the great hall of the Massassi temple to celebrate their triumph. Luke, Han and Chewbacca strode through the assembled ranks to a high dais, where Princess Leia stood waiting with General Dodonna and the other Rebel

Concept art for the presentation ceremony in the Massassi Temple on Yavin 4.
RALPH MCQUARRIE

leaders. C-3PO looked on, accompanied by the newly repaired and gleaming R2-D2.

With a proud smile, the Princess awarded the Medal of Bravery to Han and Luke. As cheers echoed from the walls, the heroes turned to face the assembled crowd. The Empire was not yet defeated; but the Rebels had struck a mighty blow in the name of peace, justice and freedom throughout the galaxy.

Artists

An early poster concept featuring versions of Luke Skywalker, Han Solo, Chewbacca, R2-D2 and C-3PO. RALPH MCQUARRIE

RALPH MCQUARRIE, born in Indiana in 1929, was a legend in the field of conceptual illustration. McQuarrie produced concept paintings for *E.T.: The Extra-Terrestrial*, the original *Battlestar Galactica* television series, all three films in the classic *Star Wars* trilogy, and the movie *Cocoon*, for which he won an Academy Award for Visual Effects. Prior to his career in film production, McQuarrie worked as a technical illustrator at Boeing. After partnering with young filmmaker George Lucas, he painted scenes from Lucas's second draft script that informed the design direction of the film. In doing so he helped create some of the most iconic characters in movie history, including C-3PO, R2-D2, and Darth Vader. McQuarrie's paintings have been reproduced as collectible posters and prints, and his original artworks have appeared in museum exhibitions, including the wildly popular touring show *Star Wars: The Magic of Myth*. He passed away in 2012.

JOE JOHNSTON is an award-winning film director and effects artist whose directorial career includes classics such as *Honey, I Shrunk the Kids*, *The Rocketeer*, *Jumanji*, *October Sky*, and *Captain America: The First Avenger*. Born in Austin, Texas, Johnston attended California State University Long Beach and the Art Center College of Design before working as a storyboard artist and special effects art director on the first *Star Wars* trilogy. At Lucasfilm, Johnston worked closely with George Lucas to develop designs for now-iconic vehicles and characters and wrote a children's book starring the Ewoks from *Return of the Jedi*. After the *Star Wars* trilogy wrapped, Johnston attended the University of Southern California film school as a step toward developing his own directorial skills and served as associate producer on George Lucas's 1988 film *Willow*. Johnston, who won an Academy Award for Best Visual Effects for his work on *Raiders of the Lost Ark*, has continued his moviemaking career as director of the 2013 thriller *Not Safe for Work*.

JOHN BARRY was a British production designer hired by George Lucas to design and build the sets for *Star Wars* – for which he received an Academy Award. He designed the box-office hits *Superman* and *Superman II*, before being hired as second-unit director on *The Empire Strikes Back*. Tragically, he died of meningitis during production.

IVOR BEDDOES was a British sketch artist and designer who contributed storyboards to *Star Wars* and *The Empire Strikes Back*, as well as many other productions. During the Second World War he served as a draughtsman in the Royal Signal Corps, and went on to work designing sets, costumes and titles for a series of films by Michael Powell and Emeric Pressburger. He passed away in 1981.

JOHN BERKEY studied at the Minneapolis School of Art and worked as a freelance artist from the 1960s onwards. He developed a reputation as a specialist in science-fiction illustration, creating covers for novels by authors like Isaac Asimov, Philip K. Dick, and Robert Heinlein. George Lucas was inspired by Berkey's paintings, and in 1976 commissioned him to create some of the first poster art for *Star Wars*. His iconic artwork would be used for the UK cover of the official novelisation, *Star Wars: From the Adventures of Luke Skywalker*. He passed away in 2008.

ALEX TAVOULARIS is an art director, draughtsman and illustrator who contributed storyboards to *Star Wars*. His film credits include *Peggy Sue Got Married*, *Apocalypse Now*, *King of New York* and *The Godfather Part III*. As a fine artist, his paintings and drawings have been exhibited in Paris and Germany.

Concept art for a stormtrooper on the Death Star. RALPH McQUARRIE

Concept art for the exterior of the Death Star, with the *Millennium Falcon* entering the docking bay. RALPH MCQUARRIE